Koyote Millar & Rahul Sen (eds.)

Queers in Quarantine

Anthology

First published 2023 by Mohini Books

www.mohini.no

ISBN 978-82-93637-08-0 (Print)

ISBN 978-82-93637-09-7 (E-book)

Table of contents

Acknowledgements 4
Introduction: A dialogue across distances and differences 6
Alonely 24
the anatomy of dialogue 25
Pensive 29
Notes from 2020 30
Tears & Breath 61
cell-u-loss 64
my mind at midnight 66
Pandemia humana 67
How I Inherited the Habit of Burying Sadness 72
Our home holds us 75
DoorsBang 76
Photo series: "Masks Unify Us" 78
The Motorcycle Diaries 85
Flight 93
Poems for Anurag 95

A Queer Narrative 104
Fruiting 117
Contributors 118

Acknowledgements

We are profoundly grateful to everyone who took the time to submit their words and their art in response to the call for this project. Thank you for sharing your creativity and craft! Thank you also for your patience with the editing and coordinating process. An extra shout out to those of you who asked gently for signs of life and progress along the way when we went radio silent for too long, it helped us dig ourselves back out from other tasks and keep inching towards completion.

Much gratitude to our wider Mohini & QiQ team: Thank you Anwesh Sahoo for the captivating and beautiful cover. Thank you Davide Bertelli and Andrew Cook-Jolicoeur for generous and meticulous proofreading. Not least, thank you Vikram and Stefan for making Mohini Books in the first place, inviting us in as editors on this project, and balancing trust and support.

Thank you all old and new Mohini friends who have given us energy by voicing your enthusiasm for this project, and volunteering your time and skills for future projects. We look forward to them!

But first, we look forward to sitting down with *Queers in Quarantine*, sniffing its new book smell (or giving the screen an extra clean) and exploring all the contributions again as we share them with you, and you share them with your friends, lovers and networks, and we all re-discover ourselves and each other in new, painful, joyful, expansive ways.

Introduction: A dialogue across distances and differences

Koyote Millar & Rahul Sen

"Do not be afraid; our fate

Cannot be taken from us; it is a gift."[1]

Thank you, dear reader, for your curiosity and attention in picking up this collection of queer voices, reflections and perspectives on loss, longing, letting go and learning to live in new ways through the Covid-19 pandemic.

In early June 2021, Mohini Books sent out a call asking for poems, written or graphic short stories, erotica, articles, black-and-white photoessays or personal narratives from people who identify as queer, reflecting experiences with the pandemic, lockdowns and quarantine. Many of us know something about the cost of feeling isolated and alone, and the importance of being able to imagine and reach for community in the face of sudden crisis. In the Mohini team, the Covid-19 pandemic created a need to check in with our extended queer community – to invite mutual support and expression, to be scared, confused and make new sense together. So we asked – and we received. So much richness in the midst of all the pandemic-related loss and restrictions. What a gift.

---

1 Alighieri, Dante. *The Inferno,* 6. Translated by John Cardi [1954]. First Signet Classics, 2009

As editors, we, Rahul and Koyo, have had the double joy of experiencing and reading and spending time with each submission in several rounds. We have talked about them individually and collectively over email and video with each other, also with the artists and authors, and with the proofreaders. In both editing and proofreading, it has been our priority to honour and clarify the particular vision, voice and preferences of the maker, and acknowledge our varied and different experiences, locations, perspectives, intersections, and expressions under the queer umbrella – or parasol.

True to its big queer, messy heart, our anthology – Queers in Quarantine *– has been a slow-burning, co-created labour of love, with much learning by doing. It is born out of dialogue over email and video, long pauses, mutual patience, prodding and sudden swirls of activity in the spaces between – and has emerged in parallel with many other projects, commitments, and sudden happenings, including Covid-19 illness for some of us.*

We are very excited to finally share our collective effort with everyone who has been waiting for the finished anthology, and with anyone who stumbles over it and suddenly feels less alone, more at home, curiously confused, provoked and enlightened, all of the above or none of the above and entirely your own response.

Quite early on in the process we talked about what sort of introduction we wanted to write, and discussed various possible formats. We tried several. In the end, it feels in keeping with all the dialogue and continuous reflection and learning that has been part of this project to also have the introduction as a dialogue, and one that is more about reflections and daring to ask questions than it is about having answers – we will have to keep figuring those out together. So welcome to this queer conversation, and to both cacophony and clarity.

Rahul: Two years into the Covid-19 pandemic, I have been wondering: What could it mean to read the cantos of Dante's *Inferno* from *The Divine Comedy* (1308-21) in a pandemic or a post-pandemic world?

As the Roman poet Virgil escorts Dante through the nine concentric circles of Hell, the latter faints for he cannot bear the horrid and putrid sight of death, pestilence, decay, blood, pus, tears, and gore that constitute Hell. By the third canto, Dante collapses and faints as the wailing of the damned souls enters his ears; he does not regain his consciousness until he is ferried across the river Acheron to the other side. Dante seems poetically to suggest that the excruciating horrors and torturous sight of Hell are unbearable, unintelligible, and unthinkable by the ordinary senses of the human mind and the everyday sense of self. Consequently, the mind has to switch itself off as Dante loses his consciousness once it encounters the gut-wrenching realities of the Inferno. One could say Dante was lucky to be able to switch off his mind. What if the mind is compelled to keep witnessing the ghastly realities of Hell, left teetering on the brink of a precipice, on the verge of losing itself at any moment?

I think all of us who have survived the past two years of pandemic have been confronted with realities and vulnerabilities we might have preferred to switch off, ignore or "unsee". In India, we witnessed an exponential rise in cases of infection alongside an acute shortage of oxygen, a dearth of hospital beds, and inadequate vaccine supplies, all contributing to high death tolls. Shutting off our minds was not an option even when the world around us was metamorphosing into a cataclysmic inferno.

Koyo: I see your point. And I have been thinking along similar lines, not with reference to Dante, but with reference to the work I do as a therapist to support people in healing and transforming harrowing and traumatic experience, and the effects over time of being stuck in a situation your whole system desperately wants to avoid or escape. When I read your reflections I am also strongly reminded of how different the pandemic experience has been in different parts of the world, for example in Norway and in India. Which in turn points to all sorts of big topics concerning the unfair distribution of resources and consequences, and the dire need for more equity and justice in the world. The pandemic is global, but our individual experiences and perspectives are local. It feels important to acknowledge that the complexity of queer experience during the pandemic is much greater than the scope of this anthology, but I like how the texts and images here reflect both commonalities and differences in pandemic and queer experiences, with contributors situated in different places and speaking from a diversity of backgrounds and perspectives. And I think that a common theme that stands out in the anthology, and that we have also witnessed in the various queer networks and communities we are engaged with, is an impressive level of creativity and resilience in the face of horror and loss.

Rahul: Yes, I agree. In India, the government declared a stringent lockdown and the less privileged lost their jobs overnight: the daily wage labourers, the migrant workers, the domestic helpers, the small retailers and shopkeepers impacted by both the virus and the callous, apathetic government. The more privileged were quarantining within the safety of their homes, which were perhaps not so safe at all. Many queer and transgender people – and many others who do not meet the conservative expectations of the self-proclaimed moral brigade – regularly had to confront harassment and abuse from their own family. News reports described how domestic violence increased during the quarantine period, while mental health declined.

Outside, the din and bustle of the streets had disappeared. In Indian cities, the loneliness of the roads was occasionally interrupted by the honking of ambulances that signalled yet another death or another number being added to the government records of those being hospitalized. In short, the larger picture was dismal. There was danger both outside and inside the house and it left many people with nowhere to go. There was an overwhelming sense of loss from which nobody was immune.

Koyo: The loss of work and important forms of safety, or relative safety, at least, and the sense of "nowhere to hide" or "nowhere to go" had a huge impact here too. Though I have been so incredibly grateful for the fact that during the lockdowns in Oslo we could still go outside, as long as we could keep enough distance from each other, which is possible here. Of course, there were many people who also avoided going outside because they were afraid of potential sources of infection, and many of them have struggled with "coming out" again once that was possible. For those who also basically had to "go back in the closet" in various ways during the pandemic because of where they were living or who they were living with, having to "come out" again has had many layers to it.

To what you say about overwhelming loss, I want to add that both in editing this anthology and in my own life, I have been struck by how, in the midst of loss, there can also be such unexpected gifts: beautiful expressions of care, new friendships and forms of connection, new openings for self-reflection and self-expression, important reminders and creative reclamations of being where previously there has been constant and frantic doing. In the aftermath of the several waves of the pandemic, I think some of us are mourning our dead and our losses, some of us are marvelling at new life and loves, and some are doing this in equal measure. Pain and resilience, vulnerability and possibility, and limitations and privilege are all explored in this anthology and have all been spelled out for us in new ways during this pandemic. I also think several of the contributions show how our experiences during the pandemic invite us, or maybe require us, to live differently and make new sense of our lives.

Rahul: I like your point about "coming out" – it has a double connotation in the Covid context. Coming out of the closet and coming out from the home. Both imply a risk, and as you rightly say, both compel us to find new ways of living!

To think more about new ways of living, I want to draw attention to a text by Sigmund Freud. In his 1917 essay "Mourning and Melancholia", Freud argues that there are at least two different attitudes to loss that a person may exhibit. In one instance, "the reaction to the loss of a loved person, or to the loss of some abstraction which has taken the place of one, such as one's country, liberty, ideal, and so on," (243)[2] is what he calls mourning. In Freud's understanding, mourning is neither pathological nor requires any medical intervention: it is a psychic process, whereby the person undergoes a period of grieving. As the work of mourning is completed, the ego which was so strongly attached to the lost object becomes "free and uninhibited" (245) once again. Contrarily, the second attitude to loss, which Freud characterizes as melancholia, is more complicated. In this case, the person grieves the loss of a dear object but does not quite know what exactly is lost. Freud uses the example of a jilted lover to explain the workings of a melancholic mind. He writes:

> ...the object has not perhaps actually died, but has been lost as an object of love... In yet other cases, one feels justified in maintaining the belief that a loss of this kind has occurred, but one cannot see clearly what is it that has been lost, and it is all the more reasonable to suppose that the patient cannot consciously perceive what he has lost either. This, indeed, might be so even if the patient is aware of the loss which has given rise to his melancholia,

2 Freud, Sigmund. *On Murder, Mourning, and Melancholia.* United Kingdom: Penguin Books Limited, 2005. Print.

> but only in the sense that he knows whom he has lost but not what he has lost in him (245)[3].

To put it simply, mourning is directed towards an exact object, whereas melancholia is disoriented and does not quite know what it has lost.

My reasons to invoke Freud's essay in the context of the Covid-19 pandemic are two. It is a well-known fact that the Covid-19 pandemic has denied many people the right to mourn in conventional ways. The usual mourning process surrounding a death has been fragmented, postponed or derailed. Children were not allowed to see their dying parents, people were prohibited by overloaded and understaffed hospitals from visiting their infected partners and spouses who might be on ventilation, struggling for their last breath. In India, even after death, the bodies of the deceased were not handed over to the family. They were sent to a separate crematorium where only two family members were allowed to enter. So many of my friends, acquaintances, and relatives helplessly sobbed and cried while recounting that they were not allowed to see their loved ones for "one last time", could not touch their near and dear ones "one last time." This particular phrase – "one last time" – featured, and still continues to feature in so many Covid-related conversations: "could not see for *one last time*," "could not talk for *one last time*," "could not touch for *one last time*."

---

[3] Ibid.

I have a distinct impression that the pandemic realities and restrictions denied many people a sense of closure in their relationship with the deceased. Consequently, the bereaved could not adequately mourn and make sense of their losses. The grief just piled up inside, more and more burdensome, with no real outlet or release. In addition to this, there were all the other losses – of important communities, of cherished activities, of dreams. I suspect that many of us came out of the Covid-19 pandemic both in unresolved mourning and suffused with melancholia. We know something about who or what we have lost while simultaneously not exactly knowing what was lost to us, or what those losses mean to our sense of self and our sense of ourselves in our surroundings. In the absence of normal strategies and rituals to support mourning and closure, the grief has nowhere to go, and can remain crippling and confusing for much longer. That was my first reason to invoke Freud in this context.

Koyo: I think that is an interesting application of Freud's ideas on grief and melancholia, and again, you really highlight how brutal the pandemic experience has been in the places with the highest rates of infection and the most deaths. It makes me want to think more about how this combination of grief and melancholia is still making itself felt and known for people in different places and in different ways. My impression is that, for many of us, it intertwined with another source of anxiety and loss: changes in climate and wildlife that are increasingly difficult to ignore and deny, even for those of us who have previously had the dubious privilege of being able to carry on as usual and distract ourselves by all manner of means. It is also my experience, both personally and as a therapist, that one consequence of not quite knowing what is lost, is that it often makes *us* feel lost or at a loss. Which in turn can easily drive us anxiously to cast about for something or someone that seems more defined and manageable to blame. I wonder what we can all do for ourselves and for each other in the aftermath of this pandemic to support the transformation of melancholia and "lostness" into a grief that feels more possible to process and act on in healing and meaningful ways. What is your second reason to invoke Freud's essay in the context of Covid-19 and this anthology?

Rahul: My second reason has to do with the way in which queerness often has to engage with, and has historically engaged with, the question of loss. If the first wave of the modern queer movement in America, and I use the word *queer* loosely here because they did not call themselves that, was an uprising and rebellion against police brutalities and police raids, then the second major political mobilization of queer people was in response to the Aids epidemic crisis in the eighties and nineties. This crisis pushed new numbers of people from many groups under the queer umbrella into collaborating to fight a deadly virus and a callous, homophobic government that blamed "the gays" for spreading the virus. Several recent cultural texts, like Ryan Murphy's 2014 film *The Normal Heart* (2014) and the 2018 – 2021 web series *Pose,* depict the harrowing experiences of the Aids epidemic among gay men, and in communities of queer and transgender people of colour. One can easily draw analogies between the Aids epidemic crisis and the Covid-19 pandemic. There are significant differences between the two, but also common threads in attitudes to the virus and in the public response to the question of loss.

The ostracization of infected people by their families, the absence of medication, the slow death caused by the illness that created an atmosphere of terror, violence, morbidity, and an overwhelming sense of loss. With Aids, the authorities branded the disease as "gay cancer" and pointed to the "promiscuous gay lifestyle" as the cause of the outbreak of the disease. In the absence of medicine and treatment, a prohibition on sex was proposed as a solution by the powers that be to check the epidemic. I have written extensively about the sexual and political implications of these gestures in an article that was published during the initial months of the Covid-19 pandemic, titled "Virus Fetish, Viral Desire," that also explores the phenomena of coronavirus porn and quarantine porn, and I do not wish to repeat that argument here.[4]

What I would like to highlight here, and with reference to Freud's analysis of loss and mourning and meaning, is how creative responses to loss have structured queer subjectivity post the Aids epidemic crisis. Sometimes even in ways that can seem unintelligible to people not much affected by the brutal realities of that crisis. In his book *Unlimited Intimacy*, Tim Dean engages with the gay subcultural practice of barebacking, bug-chasing, and gift-giving wherein unsafe anal sex is performed with consent between HIV positive and HIV negative people. This is a practice that aims to rupture the exceptional state of virus infection and envisions

---

4 Sen, Rahul. "Virus Fetish, Viral Desire." *Raiot.* 31 March 2020. Web. 03 June 2022.

creating a community of the infected. The virus is seen as a "gift" that is transmitted from one person to another. One can, of course, argue that this self-annihilating gesture could be read as what Sigmund Freud would characterize as the "death drive." I believe that this subcultural practice can also indicate ways in which people make sense or come to terms with the question of loss. At the heightened moment of the Aids epidemic when friends and lovers were dying every day, nobody had solution to the problem posed by the virus. Loss seemed inevitable and just a matter of time. The threat of infection ushered in a new form or mode of life for many queer people; each one of them tried to imagine it uniquely. In such a moment, and denied the right and support to mourn the loss of their loved ones, a section of homosexual men attempted to create a new meaning out of their loss by playing around creatively in ways that helped them survive with a sense of agency, community and meaning, even though it was physically risky.

Koyo: I am listening. You are making some provocative and thought-provoking connections. Maybe even creating a framework for a whole new anthology that someone reading this might be inspired to edit? Both in connection to the "death drive" and the need to create a sense of meaning and agency in the face of overwhelm I am now thinking of the rhetoric and behaviours we have heard and seen during the pandemic, including from people who actively identify as anti-vaxers and anti-mask. I have always been interested in how behaviours that can seem confusing or destructive at first glance can suddenly make sense as "meaning-making" and somehow "supportive of self" when you grasp the full context they have arisen in response to and play out in. On a slightly different note, but also with reference to some of the early rhetoric around and public response to Aids, I have to say that a lot of media coverage of the new monkeypox outbreak is along depressingly familiar and moralizing lines. Am I also correct in hearing you suggest that queer responses to the question of loss vis-à-vis the Aids epidemic crisis could provide an interesting lens on a range of reactions and responses during the recent pandemic? I am certainly also now thinking about how the queer community managed to respond creatively with activism, art, collaborative efforts and mutual support in response to the Aids crisis. And that historical queer creativity in the face of loss may have something to teach us on how to engage with the excruciating pain and pervasive sense of loss that the Covid-19 pandemic has brought about for many.

Rahul: Yes, I think looking at queer strategies for survival and meaning during the Aids crisis, with all the horror and loss it involved, can be useful, enlightening and maybe in some ways inspiring in our current pandemic times. And after all, this anthology was an effort on our part, however miniscule, to create queer community at a time when many individuals were distanced and separated from one another.

Koyo: This is true, and the editorial process of putting the anthology together offered much richness in the midst of all the pandemic-related restrictions.

Rahul: Yes, and what a gift it has been! If the barebackers sought to create a community of the infected through the "gift" of the virus, we attempted to build a community through the gift of words and visuals. These words and visuals infected us with the impossible hope to survive in the face of relentless losses.

Koyo: Woah, this comparison makes me so uncomfortable that I suspect there are all sorts of interesting layers to investigate and unpack in my own response. You are good at these provocative analogies! I also want to take a moment to explicitly celebrate all the pieces in this anthology as in themselves creative responses to restriction and loss. Plus I want to re-read and re-look at their specific content through this sort of "creative responses to loss" lens. It is a slight change of topic, but in your reflections on both Dante's Inferno and the Aids crisis you have mentioned the horror of being unable to avoid witnessing disease and death. It is my impression that the Covid-19 pandemic has poked a lot of us right in our existential anxiety around suffering, disease and death in new ways that can't easily be ignored, and some of the pieces in the anthology also touch on this. What are your thoughts on this, and especially in the context of living queer lives?

Rahul: I think one can say with certainty that the Covid-19 pandemic has made most people of this generation much more aware of death. Jacqueline Rose's article titled "Living Death," published in *Gagosian Quarterley* in 2020 opens with these lines:

> What exactly is being asked of people when they are told to "stay at home" or "self-isolate" in response to the covid

> threat? In a recent BBC Panorama report on women who have managed to escape their abusers during lockdown, one woman was asked, "What did the 'stay at home' message mean to you?" "Death," she replied almost inaudibly, and then repeated the word as if not expecting to be heard.[5]

This unpredictability and abruptness of death has become more common in the face of the pandemic. It is intriguing to note, however, that unpredictability, unverifiability, uncertainty have more structural affinities with queerness that many may imagine. For one thing, the brutal truth is that queer people have historically lived with closer proximity to death and often still do. In the United States there has been an epidemic of lethal violence against transwomen of colour, and on 12 June 2016, a mass shooting took place at Pulse, a queer nightclub in Orlando, Florida, that left 49 people killed and 53 others wounded. One could say that the Covid-19 pandemic has turned the tables around and made the terror and suddenness of death a far more generalizable experience.

Koyo: Yes, maybe so – though I am not sure yet what this means for queer lives and loves. In the same month that we were writing this introduction, a shooting took place outside Norway's most well-known gay bar that left two people dead and 21 others wounded. The attack led to the cancellation of the official Oslo pride march by the organizers, and the police recommended the

---

[5] Rose, Jacqueline. "Living Death." *Gagosian Quarterly*. Winter 2020 Issue. 09 May 2021. Web.

cancellation of several other pride events in Oslo and around the country because of a "heightened level of threat against the queer community" that is still ongoing. Many of us marched through Oslo in a pride parade anyway, and participated in both public and more private events to reclaim our streets and reach out and support each other in different ways. Once again trying to respond creatively as individuals and a community to sudden loss and a lack of official support for how grief, anger and fear needed to be acknowledged and addressed. I could say a lot about this, but it honestly feels too fresh, and I also risk taking us too far away from the scope and focus of this introduction. I think it is soon time for us to hand the microphone to the contributors and let their rich and eloquent voices, drawings and photos speak for themselves. Let's just say that none of what has recently happened in Oslo makes queer resilience and creativity in the face of risk, fear and loss feel any less relevant.

Rahul: I would also argue that queerness is intimately aware of and in dialogue with uncertainty and liminality, states of transition rather than positions of security. Many major queer theorists like Judith Butler, Eve Kosofsky Sedgwick, Lee Edelman, among others, have repeatedly argued that queerness is that which often escapes definite and singular positions. It is to be found in the in-between and liminal spaces that inform our lives and loves. Queerness does not confirm anything, neither does it come with any guarantee – of desire, sexuality, or gender. It is a space where old meanings are relinquished and re-formed, erased and overlapped at every instance. In this, the uncertain times that we are occupying at the moment mirror the impulses that organize and structure queerness. Maybe it is due to this reason that, in almost all the contributions to this anthology, pleasure and pain, loss and joy, love and betrayal, happiness and sadness, seem to co-exist and tussle with one another.

Koyo: I like this point. For me, at least, queerness is certainly about not shying away from pain and complexity, but instead celebrating or at least living creatively with the reality that many things can co-exist that are often presented as mutually exclusive and binary. Life is often paradoxical. Within uncertainty and liminality there is always possibility. That is something I definitely see explored and reflected in this anthology. As you say, a lot of "and" rather than "or". A lot of clarity, liveliness and patience in the face of suffering, mortality and confusion.

Can I say on behalf of both of us that our encounters and exchanges in the making, editing and proofing of the anthology have offered new inspiration, insight and learning? The contributions reflect how queer lives in the pandemic have had commonalities and big differences in different locations. Some of these differences invite renewed and painful awareness about the deeply entrenched and flawed power dynamics in the world, and a very unjust distribution of resources and cost in the face of global challenges. So once again, how can we keep acting on this awareness in new and useful ways with care, creativity and courage? What can we let go and grieve, and what can we take with us and nourish? I know we will need friendliness, and we will need trust. We will need to acknowledge our differences and our interdependence. As always, we will need each other!

Rahul: Indeed: This is truly queerness as a way of life!

Alonely

Minal Hajratwala

Our niece, when asked if someone helped her with a drawing, says proudly, beaming, "No! I did it *alonely*!" Now it's a word we say, *alonely,* as in: *Oh you're sitting here alonely?* Or, *Do you want company* (to the store, on an errand) *or would you rather go alonely?* You and I broke up, we're broken up, we did that whole breakup thing, but somehow we're still in the same apartment, 2 bedrooms 2 bathrooms, meeting in the middle on the twin Lazyboys or rubbing elbows in the small kitchen, and it's me you wake when another loved one dies, you and the dog sitting on the edge of my single bed weeping, and it's you I turn to when my mindknots get so tangled I can't solve them, so despite the breakup and then the long months of pandemic, neither of us is ever alone, so much so that often I crave solitude, the deep uninterrupted quiet of living alone, the long sinking into dreamscape and selfstory time and moving room to room around the house without another voice slashing through my thoughts. I long for and know sometime soon I'll have the kind of exhale, long and green, that I feel only when I'm truly deeply alone in a space that is (at least a while) my own. I don't think I'll ever be the sort who seeks out others just for diversion or re-juicing. Still, in these grieftimes deathtimes terrortimes hatetimes survivaltimes, how fortunate, how grateful, how glad I've felt not to have to do it all *alonely.*

the anatomy of dialogue

Martine Johansen

I notice different things now

like the Sikh bus driver listening to Punjabi radio
Guru Granth Sahib maybe
I don’t speak Punjabi
maybe he is listening to a standup comic
whoever might be the Indian incarnation of Steve Martin

I don’t know
but I do notice

I listen more
we all do we are forced to
we don’t speak through the face masks

we smile only with our eyes

reminding ourselves of the anatomy of dialogue

the stock and supply of wordwork

conversing solely by way of a fleeting glimpse

peeping in-between shelves in supermarkets

we are learning to use our corneas and irises

to articulate all things the sum of it

two eyes
two ears
one mouth covered

the mathematics of interpersonal transmission introspection infection

a sense of interpretation heightened

- hi, can I sit here?

a question is spoken by way of a glance and dilation of the pupils

easily confused with *- I love you*

easily confused with *- will you hold me?*

easily confused with *- can you see me? I mean <u>really</u> see me?*

we communicate differently

I suppose I don't know but I do notice

the eyes of others seeking out a conversation

a connection blinking out in Morse code

- is this really happening?

- are we breathing poisoned air?

- have you shared breath with someone infected?

- are you safe?

- have you been tested?

- can I take you home?

- are you sure I can't take you home with me?

Pensive

Subhajit Sikder

A note on the drawing: The lockdown was an intense suspended period of paranoia, regrets, likeability, and eroticism with myself and my body. During the pandemic lockdown, we collectively experienced physical confinement, temporal slowdown, and multiple forms of uncertainties. At the centre of all of this was the human body. So when the lockdown was announced I was hit by an avalanche of paranoia with my body. The result was that I was washing my hands after touching every new thing. I felt the immense need to take care of it. But it wasn't just that I began imagining my body in all the forms that it could have been. I reflected on all the times when I took my own body for granted. It was when I decided to discover myself, my multiple identities, my multiple limits and reaches, the perfections and imperfections of my body. I discovered a certain likeability to myself, to my body. This artwork represents all of that. But most importantly it tries to portray my discovery of my queer self and my body, of my respecting and liking my body and myself a little more.

Notes from 2020

Asad Ali Zulfiquar

The pandemic was a call for me to slow down, minimize and do less – something that I had to learn for the first time, after spending a long period of my life living and working in cultures of speed.

The change that this time required of me and my family were things that could only seep into our daily lives through patient, conscious practice. Caring is one of those changes, a primal skill, and need of the hour. Yet like many of us, I only had an abstract idea of what it is, influenced by the noise of advertisements commodifying and selling care and wellness to us.

I had lost my job, and looking for work during a virus outbreak was counterproductive as it only added to my stress. The task of caring required letting go of my ideas of what care looked like before the pandemic, centering my body and listening to its needs, and coming up with ways of meeting them that I had either forgotten or not known before.

With no exits this time, the home, the body, and the family became the only site of work, love, rest, and change. Writing has been a great tool and practice for my well-being. My notes, letters and journal entries offer documentation of my attempts at creating ways of remembering, recognizing, returning, redeeming, recovering, and resting – first-hand insights into finding the locus of change, so I could arrive at a position to care for others.

To share it with you, I draw strength from these words, let them sink in and set me in motion.

"But these truths were a fire in me then. I can say them now, without getting burnt." (11)

— Frantz Fanon, *Black Skin, White Masks*[6]

"So it is better to speak

remembering

we were never meant to survive."

— Audre Lorde, *A Litany for Survival*[7]

---

[6] Fanon, Frantz. (1986). Black Skin, White Masks. Pluto Press.

[7] Lorde, Audre. (1977). https://www.poetryfoundation.org/poems/147275/a-litany-for-survival

“Speak

Speak, your lips are free,

speak, your tongue is still yours,

your slim body is yours alone,

speak, this life is yours, still yours.”

— Faiz Ahmed Faiz, *Bol/Speak*[8]

Here is an email excerpt

that you can reply to, too

Jan 2020

"... it gets super lonely because not many people share your conception of connection then, like I've mentioned" – sufithoughts to lightermachis · 12:55 PM · 1/17/2020 · Instagram DM

8 https://allpoetry.com/poem/8542605-Speak-by-Faiz-Ahmed-Faiz

I'm curious to know your conception of connection. Feel free to be the first to share.

Change ways of relating

by softening the gaze,

Jan 2020

Every time I'm in a pickle, I make sure I sit and listen to know what's up. I make sure I eat. I make sure my room is clean and my clothes are ready. I hold myself with a soothing touch if I'm upset. I speak gently. I don't speak cruelly. I use my skills to solve my problems. In the moment, I do everything I could ask from a friend, a lover. In the moment, I am everything I could ask from a friend, a lover. I changed many things to reach a point where I'm ready to accept the tender loving care I can offer to nurture my wounded spirit and survive acts of lovelessness.

softening touch,

and extending it to material surfaces that touch me

Jan 2020

I don't always make my bed before leaving, because I come home daily to a bed made by my mother. Today, before leaving, I took a hard look at it. I know it won't matter if I don't make my bed because I'll still be returning to a bed that's been made. But what if it does matter? What if it matters how I treat my bed? I don't really like it, because it's not the softest bed in the world. I often wake up feeling irritated by it. It's never been big enough either. Yet I spent most of my time in it. Today, before leaving, I paused for a moment and made my bed. I did that as gently and slowly as I could. Once tidied, I gently placed my palm on the bed and offered gratitude for carrying me all this time. What if one extended kindness to inanimate objects, and held them as tenderly as one wants to be held – not because they may break upon manhandling, but because our treatment of things that touch us changes us? How would my life differ if I carried the things that carry me with care, just as I wish to be carried?

to immaterial spaces

where touching is happening.

February 2020

My desktop is where I spend quite a lot of my time. I also treat this surface as sacred, as an altar, a place I turn to when I make prayer. It's a surface that I like to treat with kindness. A way to treat it with kindness is keeping it clean. I move the cursor on my screen slowly. I spend time lurking and writing in the paratextual spaces of the operating system. I rename files elaborately. I organize them through folders. I ensure they stay together and do not get misplaced in crowds. I change abrupt system sounds that the manufacturers set to sounds that are kinder to my ears. I pick a desktop background that invites me to look out the windows. When I decide to leave this space, I don't close the lid, putting it to sleep, leaving everything open. I do what I would do when I leave a room or a house. I close each window unhurriedly, and switch it off. Every time I return to my desktop, I return to it anew, as I wish to enter any space – anew – no piled up energy.

Here is a guide to approach hurt

with tenderness

Jan 2020

Think of the ocean's waves, never stopping no matter what you throw in it.

It sinks. The ocean is unbothered. Think of the unimaginable power of the waves to drown what you threw, as if it were nothing.

Think of the nothingness. Think of the might of the ocean.

Think of a pin cushion as if it was alive. Imagine the pain it is in. Imagine it screaming. You're hurting from the noise, because it is hurting gravely.

Will you hold on to that pain?

The kindest thing you can do to welcome your grown up self into the world, is to make room for hurt to happen upon encounter in any relationship and

not make it personal

the hurt you hold on to

is their projection of pain, of fear, of shame, of guilt, of weakness

it's theirs to begin with, not yours.

Don't make it yours. Don't keep it close to you. Don't hold on to it tightly. Let it go.

Figuring it out through friendships

Feb 2020

Create your anchors, compasses and maps. A cartography you need to keep returning to yourself, when your surroundings are hell-bent on disorienting you. Suspend the belief that feeling lost is your fault. Guide her tenderly today.

A mantra for relocation

Feb 2020

When I locate joy in something inaccessible to me, I make joy inaccessible to me. The closer I locate it to me, the more accessible it becomes.

An invite into a hard conversation

No more seeking exits

March 2020

When was the last time you had a conversation with someone that led you to change your mind about them?

Has there been a person in your life who you think is irredeemable?

Remembering all of it

especially what I would like to forget.

April 2020

I was catching up with the cousins I spent most of my childhood with. We were telling each other our earlier memories.

There were moments when I went blank. And all of them were the times when I was reminded of someone who mistreated me.

I don't remember a lot about what Arif Uncle was really like. I just remember that I didn't like him very much because he used to scold me to have dinner with the family, when I just wanted to play. I felt threatened by him, his stern face and his heavy voice. I wanted to like him, because he was handsome, made dad jokes and was such good friends with my mom and my dad. But I couldn't, knowing how his temper is. I didn't want to be subjected to that. I avoided him.

They told me about Hina Auntie. She used to be my tutor. I really enjoyed studying, but she also had a short temper and would threaten me with beating. I don't have a memory of the beating, but I do remember crying and being immensely afraid of her. I can hear her sharp voice ringing in my head, saying my name. I couldn't ever get near her, even much later. I don't think I can separate the clothes hanger from Hina Auntie. They always come up in my mind together.

Once, Sajid Uncle jolted me and lifted me up and shouted in my face. I started crying and I ran away. I was so scared. Ever since, I have never spoken to him. Not even once till this day, nor do I plan to. I really wish he didn't do that. Before that, I used to think of him as a chill uncle who would always joke around. He must have thought this was a joke too, but it didn't feel funny at all. And if it were, I wouldn't have cried and even if I did, I'd have come around, but I have never wanted to, because it wasn't a joke. It was abuse. Those who witnessed it knew that I'm never going to talk to him ever again. If it were just a joke, then maybe I would have received an apology, but I never did. It was abuse.

I don't understand why it is hard for me to recall these events, when my body remembers it all.

Here is a guide

and an obstacle course

April 2020

Rooj teaches me to embody softness by setting an example. She wouldn't hurt the beetle that would fly into the studio, but would gently pick it up and place it at the window sill for it to make its way back home. She tells us not to kill the mosquitoes in the room. She offers us to apply mosquito repellant on our skins instead, and remarks, 'There will be no violence in class.' I think of every time I've killed an insect. I think of the destructive energy that I carry along by exerting power over the powerless. I think of missed opportunities to practice softness.

She sees me through my own meanness. I struggle at it. I have found compassion lying deep inside of me, but when it comes to me, I struggle to bring it to surface, and into action. Every little thing is a challenge, a chance to enact it. She tells me it feels more natural as I continue flexing that muscle.

I apply citronella oil on my skin to challenge my instinct of killing mosquitoes now. I notice my energy shifting when I act out of irritation. One way that it is serving me is that I find it much easier now to be kind to my family while this used to be particularly challenging. The mosquitoes are teaching me how to respond gently to the hurt and the hurting. I have not been trained to be like this. So much of my life is shaped by violence that I have not known in my body how to respond differently, which makes it challenging for me to metamorphose.

I see Aang. Every time I've seen him in battle, I've seen him only deflecting his enemy's moves, dodging attacks, letting their own destructive energy bring them to their demise. Aang does not move away from his training as a monk. The thought of moving away from it puts him in an existential crisis. Nonviolence sits at his core being, and it shows in the ways he deals with challenging, and even life-threatening situations. I, on the other hand, am nothing like Aang.

Forge connections disrupted by the lockdown

with immediate surroundings

May 2020

I smelled the flowers, saw the most crimson hibiscus, and a butterfly. I held my hand as I walked.

The butterfly just sat there in an endless intimacy with the flower bud, until I dared to capture the moment in a photograph and interrupted her. Thankfully, she didn't fly too far from my slowly deteriorating eyesight that I'm only recognising now as I am unable to stretch my gaze further. I broke my glasses a few days before the lockdown.

I wonder who has been taking care of these flowers. I never found out who is responsible for taking care of this roundabout. I don't see flags or signs that mark this territory unlike the rest of the town. Just char qul[9], that are only there as ornaments, like these flowers. Except the flowers are alive and need care.

---

[9] Char Qul (The 4 Qul) are four short, protective Surahs (chapters) in The Qur'an often read or recited in prayer.

I hear many birds. I can discern at least four calls. I don't see any of them. They're small, and very quick in their attempt to skip from one tree to the other. Are they hiding? Who are they hiding from? Do they know that this may not be their home? None of them are occupying the wires today. Only some crows who watch over the place from the top of the street lights.

I just heard a rooster. I don't know why they call it the azaan. It's way past fajr. But roosters seem to call whenever they please. I remember, in school, every Urdu textbook started with a humd[10], with a reminder that these birds gather to recall God every morning, and I found that romantic.

Maybe the birds don't know what they're doing, just like me. Maybe neither of us is as random in our movements as I imagine. Maybe my imagination is limited. Maybe both, the birds and I, are moving closer to something or someone we have an affinity for when we get up every morning. Maybe that affinity is the affinity for life, for continuation. The birds have a ritual, as some Muslims do. What is my ritual?

---

10 "Azaan" is the call to prayer, "fajr" is the dawn prayer and "humd" is a praise of Allah.

with the body

June 2020

Something is slowly shifting for me. The way I look at myself in the mirror is different now than I used to. It's less punitive and judgmental now. It's gentler, softer and more affectionate.

When I'm on my own, I like to treat myself the way I want to be treated by my beloved.

The desire to code and compartmentalize my facial features, my torso, hair, gestures as masculine and feminine is leaving me, and good riddance.

I've stopped rushing while in the bathroom. When I miss the earth, I see the brownness, the softness, the warmth of my skin is so much like the earth. What a gift it is to have a body that resembles the earth.

with the wanting mind

July 2020

I did not want to stay in savasana. I wanted to get up and write. Create something. Urgently. I wanted to move and not be still. I thought of all things fleeting, the Sun, the Moon, day, night. I thought of how great these things are. They control the weather. They sustain life on earth. Everyone thinks they are important. Everyone has structured their lives around them for ages. Poets write poetry about them. They are so great. They are so loved. I want to be that great. I want to be loved. I want to be seen. I want to be important to someone other than me. So I mustn't stay in stillness. I want to catch up with the Sun, the Moon, day, night. I know I'll tire myself out. But I'm afraid if I don't try, I will be unloved, lost and forgotten. And there will be no return.

and other fragments.

June 2020

My father used to place a hundred rupee note on top of the fridge every morning before he left for work. It was for my mother to feed us all. When we grew in number and started going to school, a hundred rupee note wasn't enough and I saw my mother voicing her concern to him. On some days, he'd leave a hundred and fifty rupees. On some rare occasions, it would be as much as two hundred rupees. On some days, my mother would save twenty to fifty rupees to make us something off the regular menu. Those days would usually be the ones when we'd have guests over. People can have such different experiences and relationships with wealth that I don't know if one can be objective about it. I'm thinking of all the money I've seen you blowing away on luxuries, and I couldn't argue with you that they're unnecessary. Not everyone will get it, maybe not until they have a close encounter with poverty that changes their relationship with money.

All fragments belong

Making sense is neither prerequisite nor desired.

August 2020

There are many truths the rain reveals. here's one I noticed:

before rain, the sky carries the reflection of the earth on its body

after rain, the earth carries the reflection of the sky on its body the two remain in conversation with each other

water is the medium, light is the message, as they are in my body.

Here is a letter to my inner child

August 2020

Dear child,

I heard a clip of Firework while scrolling through the bird app, and felt my smile. It's been 10 years since that song came out. I don't know why I stopped listening to that song after a while. I guess I felt judged for it. And then I judged myself and others for it. It gave me so much joy. As I am hurting right now, very much in the same ways as you, I'm revisiting some songs you listen to. Firework is one of them. I've queued Roar.

I had a fight with my mother where I regressed a lot. She said some incredibly hurtful things to me. I kept getting hurt as I held on to them. When I heard Bad Kids, I had a moment of realisation when Gaga sings, "I'm a bad kid like my mom and dad made me." My beloved child, I am trying to see us as more than what our mom and dad made. On days when our mother attacks me, it becomes hard and I relive the pain you've felt.

I remember how much you loved the song, Hair. You felt so seen. Our parents never cut your hair, but they controlled how you presented, and threw a fit when you tried to have your way. I want to tell you that now, I decide how I want to keep my hair. You wouldn't imagine the things that I tried. I dyed my hair so many times I can't even keep track. The longest color I stayed with was green. Yes, I'm telling you that you will dye your hair green. You will also shave the sides of your head. You'll grow your hair out long. You'll get irritated and cut it short, and you'll grow it out again. And it doesn't just stop there.

Child, I know that all that you wanted when you were younger was to grow up, so you could have your way, and you will have your way. I'm currently writing to you from a time when you have had multiple jobs, some money in your bank account that I'm currently living off of in the middle of a virus outbreak, your idea of 'having it my way' will be challenged by factors beyond anyone's control, but you will not be answerable to your parents when you want to go anywhere, not even out of Karachi.

I know that neither of us know this in the body: I come to believe you and I deserve freedoms far greater than the ones Karachi grants and takes away from us.

Love,

Asad Ali Zulfiqar

Ancestral wisdom to guide

through tumultuous times

September 2020

Motia,

I brought you into my house to teach me love and care through action.

I decided to take you in when a mother was raped in front of her children and no one did anything about it. When the poor in Naya Nazimabad drowned and no one did anything about it. When Shia genocide started again and no one did anything about it. When violence begot violence begets violence will beget violence.

I brought you in to replace the poison these events have filled me with, to treat with tender loving care. This task isn't easy. I'm filled with rage and sadness. With murderous sexual violence, raging sectarian hatred, endless state brutality ravaging us all, new atrocities every day, shattered economy and starving suicidal population, this is me saying none of it is my fault. I did not build this. I do not deserve this. With daily reminders of the violence that I have inherited refreshed in my body, it is my desire and my duty to preserve my capacity to love and care for life, starting with mine and yours, and in the process, learn to live my purpose, that is to serve. I cannot serve when I'm crippled with pain. So,

I pour myself a glass of water.

I pour water in another glass.

I sing a love song.

I blow it in both the glasses.

I pour one in the flowerpot.

I drink from the other glass.

what it feels like to be guided.

October 2020

The somatic experience of looking forward. I think it was Natasha who taught me to be conscious of it. Rooj has also brought it up once as a joke, but there was truth to it. "How do you move forward?" "You take one step forward, and then another step forward."

When overwhelming thoughts and negative self-belief are pulling me back, I flag them as the trance of unworthiness. Once I've done that, I can move out of the trance and walk towards my truth. As I walk towards it, I feel what it feels like to be moving forward. The energy that is carried in my body as I keep taking footsteps forward, without feeling pulled back, or a need to look back. I feel what it feels like to not turn my back, twist my neck, pull my chin down and look down, or pull my chin towards my shoulder and look at it. I feel what it feels like to hold my head up high, what it feels like to have my eyes set to look at what's straight ahead. Feel what it feels like to have my chin parallel to the ground and notice what it is that's allowing me to keep going. Feel the pull of my truth. What is it that I'm allowing myself to be pulled by? What is the message I am receiving? Who is the messenger? What does it feel like to be the recipient of this message? What does it feel like in the body?

October 2020

remembering /ɹɪˈmɛmb(ə)ɹɪŋ/

from Latin re- "again, back to the original place" and membrum "limb, integral part of a body." Limbs help a body move. Losing them ceases movement.

remember (v). to connect the body with its limbs and move again.

remembering (n). the act of reconnecting to a lost part and setting the body in motion.

"to remember & be remembered (that is the secret)" — Shilo Shiv Suleman, "چاند humraaz"[11]

---

[11] Excerpt from a post on Instagram by artist Shilo Shiv Suleman quoting her own poetry. www.shiloshivsuleman.in and www.instagram.com/shiloshivsuleman/

"Mindful remembering lets us put the broken bits and pieces of our hearts together again. This is the way healing begins." (286)
— bell hooks, *All About Love*[12]

"…freedom is daily, prose-bound, routine

remembering. Putting together, inch by inch

the starry worlds. From all the lost collections."

— Adrienne Rich, *For Memory*[13]

Here is a recipe for a love potion

Nov 2020

pour 2 glasses of water in the vessel

light the stove

play love songs

---

[12] hooks, bell. (2018). *all about love: New Visions*. Harper Collins.
[13] Rich, A. (1993). For Memory (1979). In *A Wild Patience Has Taken Me This Far: Poems 1978-1981*. Essay, W.W. Norton.

slice some ginger

slice 1 lemon, squeeze and drop it in the boiling water

add a dash of cinnamon

dash of cardamom

dash of long pepper

dash of turmeric

a few dots of tea leaves

serve in a cup through a strainer

add 2 tablespoons of honey per cup

blow a love song before drinking

and what must be that love potion taking effect

Nov 2020

i.

Transphobia feels like poison in my body. When I'm subjected to it, it feels like poison being injected into my body, spreading through my blood. It makes my heart close up. It closes me to my own kindness. I need that kindness because mostly I'm alone and it's dangerous when I carry that poison with/in me. I don't really spend that much time with other people. Which means I'm the prime target of my own meanness. The way transphobia harms me is so insidious. It makes me relive the trauma of my own non-acceptance. What becomes of the river when someone pours poison in it. The only antidote to this poison is love – compassion, acceptance, unconditional friendliness. Anchoring myself in the experience of love that is being in my trans body, remembering what it felt like to love it by letting my trans darling love me and let it serve as a reminder when I forget. Self-compassion has been incredible to chart a map for me to find myself when I am losing me to transphobia. I reopen my heart and find myself there.

ii.

Recently, I had two very contrasting sexual encounters that taught me something about my trans identity. I thought I could simply keep it on the back burner when I'm dating, or hooking up with cis men.

I realized that I can no longer brush aside my trans identity even in casual hookups. I casually came out to this boy who didn't quite understand it, but sought to understand me with questions that felt more novice than invasive. I felt a sense of comfort and safety in my body. When we wanted to come, we masturbated. Though I didn't ask him to, he called me a beautiful woman and it made me come. I didn't realize before that someone I'm intimate with affirming my transness would help me connect with my body in ways that are also highly pleasurable. We might hook up again.

It may have been easier for me to pick up on it, because I also recently had a harrowing experience with a hookup where a cis gay man saw me, picked up on my transness and called me a transphobic slur. The rising discomfort I felt in my body after hearing it shut me off. I simply couldn't proceed with sex. My body refused to fuck him. When he came on to me, I pushed him aside with my arms, not consciously, but as a knee-jerk response. I loved how my body responded. It didn't take thinking and deciding, my body had already decided and taken charge. It must've been self-love in action.

My resistance as a trans person is rooted in my practice of self-compassion. It was almost magical to see that over time, it had become muscle memory. I think both of these experiences essentially tell me what and how my sense of belonging was broken, challenged, and how it can be nourished. That it's about time I welcome my transness to the front when it comes to seeking pleasure, and to turn to an intimate partner with empathy and trust, to invite them to understand my trans body, just as I seek understanding of their body. No more putting aside my transness for pleasure, because it's become clear to me that embracing and bringing in my transness is what I find pleasurable.

Friendships that illuminated

a dark December

Dec 2020

The trips to the police station have been cold. The police don't read my application that has all the details they need. They ask me to perform my trauma for them, repeatedly.

I don't think I want to be called over for identification every time they catch someone. I see them keeping men like rats in cages. I can see their sudden movements, the kind that are informed by guilt and shame. They're not the same people who assaulted me. They're trying to get some sleep in that cold, sunless cell. I remember staying in a room that sees no sun, permuting my sense of time, my belonging to earth. I may stop dealing with this case, because it's not being carried out on my terms. I don't want any of this. I want an acknowledgement, an apology, good nights' sleep, for me, for them. Wherever they are. I don't think the police and I are ever going to be on the same page about it.

I sat on the sidewalk at Thandi Sarak. A dog stopped by, rested her head on my knee for a while, and let me rub her belly. I'm glad I never leave the house without water. She opened my heart just enough to find there's strength in softness.

There's freedom in multiplicity:

this isn't it; there's more,

December 2020

In therapy, I learnt to talk to my emotions and know what they're trying to tell me, instead of repressing them and wishing they would go away.

Last night, I contemplated suicide.

I "know" I shouldn't, so I told myself it's illogical and completely unreasonable to think that's how I must proceed.

But it kept coming back, so I asked it what's up. "What do you really want?" It told me, "I just don't want you to go through heartbreak ever again." That was unexpected.

I was not hoping to hear that. I was expecting some self-loathing statements but there were none. Strangely, what this thought really wanted for me was protection from heartache.

I stepped into the sun. I felt the little warmth of the winter sun falling on my face. It was different from the warmth in bed under my blanket. I felt two kinds of warmth this morning, and I wondered if there were more. I reminded myself that my body is a guest house of thoughts and feelings visiting and leaving. Today, I will be a good host and not refuse entry or exit to anyone.

I went out to fetch milk. I wore only a t-shirt. I felt cold.

A man was staring at me. I felt angry. "Kya? Kya? Bol".[14] He froze. I heard a man behind him telling him, "Abay bola na tujhe nahi kia kar."[15] I felt seen, and consequently less angry.

---

14 "What? What? Say it."

15 "I've told you not to do that."

I took the first sip of my coffee. It was delicious. I felt energized.

I heard Anmol singing a Faiz couplet to me. I let it sink in. I felt soothed.

I acknowledge that I felt heartbroken last night. I acknowledge that the night is over, and a day has begun. I am ready to feel more

Tears & Breath

Jona Fedorowicz

Tears

Breath

cell-u-loss

Anil Pradhan

the plague has scorched memory such that
the water in the rice bowl is no longer water
it has become a scandal, moaning in froth
a whitish coagulated starch magma story
the art of cooking rice is an open secret
yet many tend to overlook, feign pittance
and just before getting tarred, dexterity
an annoyance to the sink of draining time
what a shame, the starch is always wasted
so thick, so gooey, with specks of the past
it reminds me of your semen on my chest
sticking to the follicles, sluicing terribly slow
this must be intolerable, sans much respite
this de(s)ta(r)ched warmth, a tell-tale disguise
perhaps a sign of desire but never of love
it's all mostly water down the chasms
for just a handful of daily sustenance
dried to perfection or stirred to a pulp
in the name of hunger, it's all but fiction

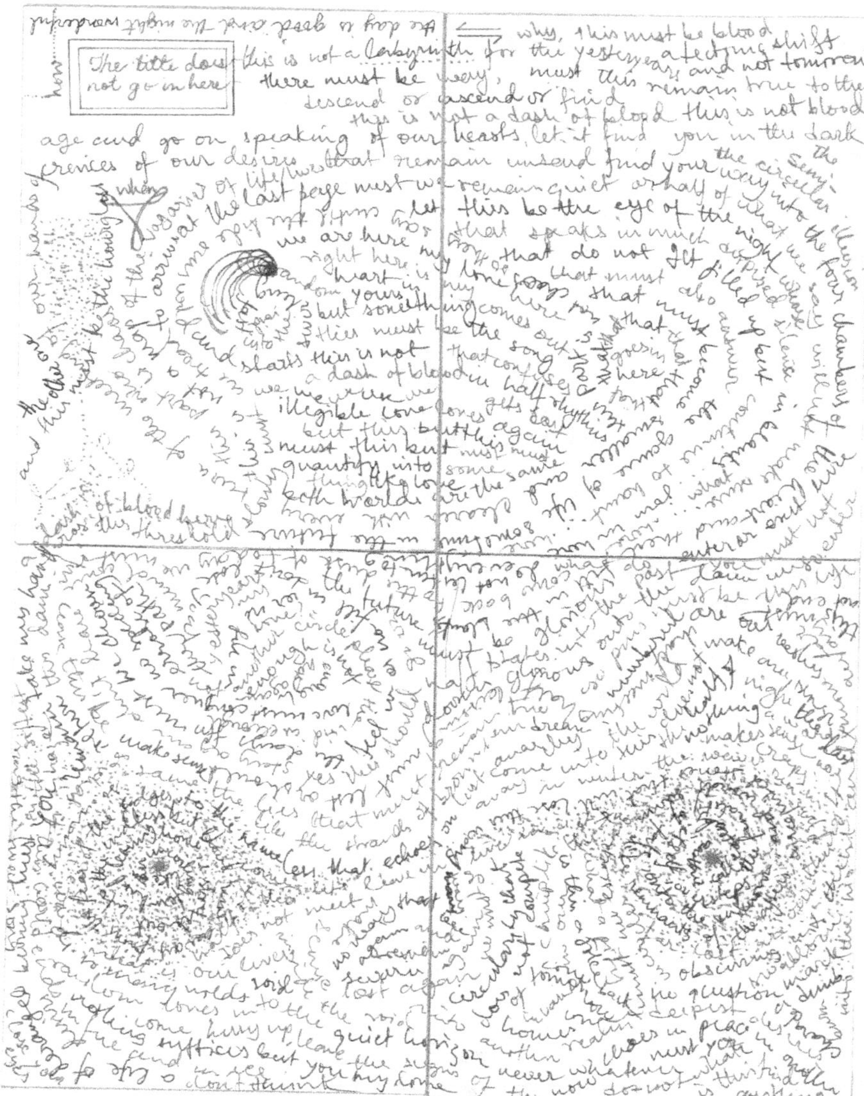

The title does not go in here
why, this must be blood
this is not a labyrinth for the yesteryears
there must be weary
must this remain true to the
descend or ascend or find
this is not a dash of blood this is not blood
age and go on speaking of our hearts, let it find you in the dark
crevices of our desires that remain unsaid find your way into the circular
let this be the eye of the night
we are here

my mind at midnight

Anil Pradhan

goes to places i never would
upon the songs of the crickets
levitates onto the cotton seams
with bricklike softness and woe
swims in the deepest blue waters
without an ounce of suffocation
swirls around the ageing house
so merciless, such enchantment
lacerates the shoulders of men
that bloody my hair, mad vines
weaves congruous tales of lies
out of pity like redressed naivety
tussles itself, shrieks, unbecomes
in the darkness, a burning riddle
floods the world with such silence
as if it were never heard before
mocks, flutters, threatens, sighs
and settles down like subtle mist
it quarantines the madness inside
an orb hovering upon a black sky
that has now stretched 457 nights

Pandemia humana

Celia Velo Camacho

Hemos logrado encender
la primavera
con nuestra ausencia,
hemos hecho cantar al campo
sin nuestras fiestas,
hemos podido escuchar
exentas del tráfico
el despertar de la naturaleza.

Antes de ayer llorábamos
en despedidas inciertas
del contacto con pieles.
Ayer estuvimos despellejado
el calor humano.
Hoy vivimos en la distancia,
en proceso deshumanizado.

Hemos aprendido a soñar,
a descansar, a pensarnos;
antes nos juzgaban por no parar,
ahora por no querer salir tanto.

Ese espejismo se desvanece,
los girasoles se marchitan tristes,
las amapolas desaparecen;
y dirán que es el verano,
pero yo digo que han visto
lo que se acontece.

Como un oasis en el desierto
que has imaginado,
como encontrar una solución
que no ha funcionado,
como fantasear un cambio
en la sociedad,
que solo ha sido un refugio,
cobarde y egoísta,
ante el peligro inminente.

Estamos celebrando,
volvemos a encontrarnos
dejando nuestra Libertad vacía
olvidándonos de nuestra cita
a las 8 con el atardecer,
naranja y rosado,
desde un prado verde.

Estamos celebrando
y, sin embargo,
quiero volver atrás
a encerrarnos,

pero no por miedo a contagiar,
sino por miedo a volver
a envenenar el ambiente.

English translation

Human pandemic

We have managed to light up
the spring with our absence,
we have made the countryside sing
without our parties,
we have been able to hear
the awakening of nature
released from the traffic.

The day before yesterday
we were mourning
with uncertain farewells.
Yesterday we were peeling away
the human warmth.
Today we live detached,
in a dehumanized process.

We have learnt to dream,
to rest, to think about ourselves.
Before, we were being judged
for not stopping,

now, we are being judged
for not wanting to go out every day.

This mirage fades,
the sunflowers wither sadly,
the poppies disappear.
People might say
that the summer is coming,
but I say that nature has seen
what is happening again.

Like an oasis in the desert
that was just your imagination,
like finding a solution
that hasn't worked,
the fantasy of a changed society
which has simply been
a cowardly and selfish refuge
from imminent danger:
Fear of death.
We are celebrating,
we are meeting our friends,
but leaving freedom empty
and forgetting our appointment
with the sunset,
orange and pink, at 8 o'clock[16].

We are celebrating and yet

---

[16] A reference to the appointment at the balconies at 8 PM for a collective applause to thank the sanitary workers during the lockdown in Spain.

I want to return
to lockdown,
not because of the fear of infecting,
but because of humans going back
to poisoning the environment
with no regrets.

Bonares, Spain, 18th of June 2020

How I Inherited the Habit of Burying Sadness

Hansika Jethnani

Learning to bury sadness was a habit. I say "was" because it is a habit I am trying to unlearn. In March 2020, when the world came crashing to a halt, so did my mind. My mind that often raced against the speed of light and always won was now drowning in its fireworks. Busyness was a coping mechanism to keep the demons in my head at bay. The stillness that life in quarantine brought, exploded in my head. Every sliver of its path trying to catch my attention. A red signal of how much intergenerational trauma my body holds.

*

I am eight, and watching my mother watch Kyunki Saas Bhi Kabhi Bahu Thi with regret. It is the same misery I see on her face everyday. As she spends her days alone, drowned in television that emotes the highest sense of patriarchy in a desi household, I imagine being like her. I want to be like her more than anything in the world because I hate going to school every morning. I cannot wait to be an adult because then I can sleep in like her. Isn't sleep equivalent to happiness? Because I've never seen her happy.

*

I am ten, and watching my father skip rice as a staple in his meal for the hundredth time. It has been four years since he has also stopped eating bread. I watch him eat, each serving a calculated portion filled with sorrow.

*

I learnt to slice bread the same way. A purposeful sliver. I learnt the language of food from watching him eat, it was a language of caution. A red light reminding me to stop more than digest.

*

I am twelve, and the house is drowning in grief. My father and mother are living in the same room, but six hundred and seventy-eight thousand miles apart. There is a pillow that divides their bodies as they sleep. It slices their silence in half.

*

When my father travelled, the weight of his absence held the house down. When he was around, the weight of his silence did. I saw more fireflies in my head than lightbulbs between them.

*

I am seventeen, and my palms are filled with sand slipping.

*

I am twenty-three, and I watch how my grandparents walk. There is a posture of silence they hold; inherited history of loss, a statue of sadness. The loss of a means of articulating their history, twisting their tongue to learn a new language. Replenishing their taste buds, wiping senses. The loss of a land is a loss of the means of accessing ancestral history. It is to speak a language only some know.

*

You see, for so long, sadness was the airbag in the car we all sat inside. It is what saved us from dying. Because to live, even as sad people, was at least a way to live. A reason to drive the car. Sadness was seeped into every fibre of our being. It is what kept us alive. But to be alive, and to live, are two different things. Burying sadness might have kept me alive. But I was not living. I did the best I knew, imitating my parents. I realise now, I buried my sadness so deeply, it only erupted when I allowed for what was in my deepest depths to surface. Allowing myself to confront my demons helped me understand the unlearning I had to do. I learnt that unpacking my trauma is the only way to break the cycle. I learnt that doing the work is painful. But necessary.

Our home holds us

Hansika Jethnani

We nestle in each other

As thunder rumbles,
politicians croak on their
lockdown guidelines
and death becomes figureless.

We roll
            into each other's slumber.

Sunrise begins with two sunny side ups

silence rests on our earlobes

orange peers into the window

until a flicker sets a fire,

and words run hastily
from our mouths.

DoorsBang

Hansika Jethnani

I look into the mirror
dripping with shame

gawking at parts of me
only you bring out.

My façade
melt
ing

Midnight nears,
and our lips lock in settled sentences

We surrender.

I am learning to love
my demons
and yours
We are both
learning
to turn them
into lions.

s
i i
R ng in love

finding its way

between shared spaces.

I left your coffee by your bedside,

you waited

to drink the cup till I returned.

Photo series: "Masks Unify Us"

Mie Cornoedus

I am living in South Korea where the problem of air pollution every winter, spring and summer is a serious threat to our health and wellbeing. We monitor air quality daily and every room in the house has air purifiers. This is where the original idea of the photos came from. The series talks about whoever you are, or however you identify, without discrimination, we all breathe the same polluted air.

Then Covid-19 struck and my mask series grew into a broader evidence of reality. From the very start of the pandemic, the authorities in South Korea called for great vigilance in preventing infection by wearing masks, inside and outside. It isn't just the ecologically aware few anymore, but absolutely everyone forcefully covering up now.

It makes me feel less of an outsider.

Masks unify us.

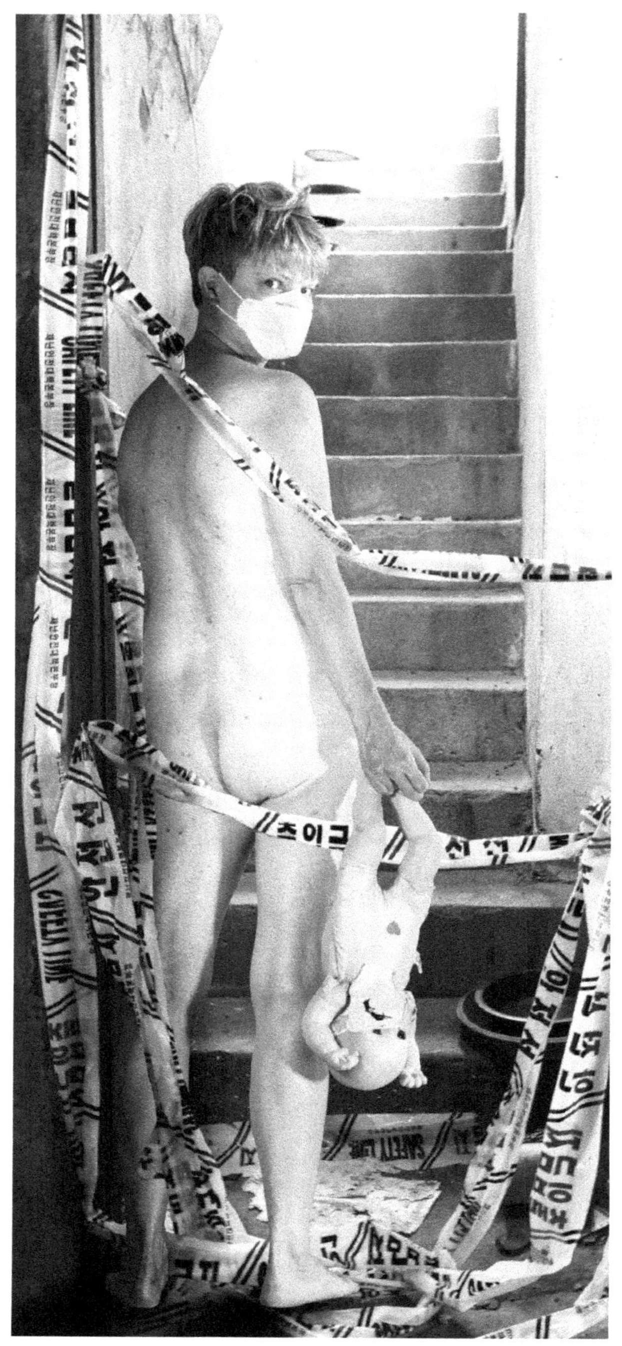
SAFETY LINE

The Motorcycle Diaries

Maisnam Arnapal

After an eighteen-hour shift amid the morbid sight and sound of the ICU, I finally got time to take some rest. When was the last time I took an eight-hour sleep? I don't even remember. It's been almost two months since the pandemic has created havoc in our lives.

Coming from a humble background, I decided to join a nursing college as it would help me get a job right after high school. Som, on the other hand, came from an affluent family. Her father was a police officer, and the rest of her family were mostly academicians and journalists. She was a voracious reader and wrote poems too. When I first visited her home, I saw the rooms decked with books in all corners. She used to talk about poverty, oppression, and freedom; recommended books and films to explore. I rarely read the books she loaned me as I got befuddled after a few pages. But I had a huge admiration for her intellect and the zeal to change the world.

While I was pursuing my Bsc Nursing in Calicut, Som and I used to text each other every day. One day I got a message, "Baby I'll join UG soon."

Never in my life had I imagined my friend, my sister, my love, Som taking up arms to fight against the state. Her idea of freedom included Manipur's freedom from India. We had corruption and massive unemployment amid a military conflict, and we all protested against them. To be part of the underground forces was never what my generation would opt for, I guessed. A part of me wanted to stop her — what if she got killed, how would she survive in the thick jungles on the Indo-Myanmar border? When she texted me she would be underground soon, I knew she had already made up her mind. How on earth could I, who was not as erudite and enlightened as her, try to convince her to change her decision?

A few months later, in February 2011, Som called me from an unknown number. She was too excited to talk to me. There was an air of confidence and command in her voice.

"Baby, the boys here call me 'Che'."

She was happy not because they addressed her as their sister in Manipuri but because she was referred to as one of her revolutionary heroes, Che Guevara. She once gave me a copy of *The Motorcyle Diaries*; she told me she was Che and I, Alberto Granado. I never read the book, but we covered many parts of Imphal and the surrounding areas on her motorcycle.

A message popped up on my phone. It was forwarded by my younger brother.

"Northeast girl spat on, called Corona."

Panicked, I opened the link. This happened in North Delhi, almost fourteen kilometres from my workplace. I hurriedly searched for similar news. There were other reports of men and women from the Northeast abused and attacked in other cities. One was denied entry into a shop in Bengaluru, some others were thrown out of their rented accommodation in Kolkata.

Som always believed the Northeast could never be a part of the Indian nation. The two are culturally and historically distinct. She found the nation-building project, a topic I learned in detail from her, fraught with violence and exclusion. Racism, as she explained to me, comes from an innate hierarchy in power. And in the current scenario, the Northeast would always be a cultural and economic inferior. I never took these words seriously, I knew there was racism faced by Northeast folks in other parts of India and within the Northeast too, how the 'outsiders' are treated. My college life in Calicut was however extremely pleasant: I couldn't recall any incident which could be termed racist. My professors and classmates were extra-protective.

When I joined a hospital as a junior nurse in Delhi, I encountered discrimination for the first time. The doctors and the patients, not all, talked to us harshly, and our work was never considered significant. I wonder whether it was a question of race, class or just being a nurse. Our salary was minimal and we could never raise our voice. We were told that it's our good fortune that we were working at a 5-star hospital (only to come back to our dorm where we spent hours cleaning, cooking, and sleeping until our next shift).

When the COVID duty began last month, we were promised an increment of ten thousand rupees per month, over and above the twenty we were already being paid. Some colleagues left for their hometown in early March, while most chose to stay back. I have colleagues from Kerala, Nagaland, and Assam – all of whom have stood the test of time.

"Hey, hope you're well. I read about attacks in Delhi. Stay safe, call me anytime."

A message from my senior, Lily, gave me some comfort. Lily is forty-five, a divorcee, mother to two kids. She has been working in Park Hospital for more than twenty years and now she is our head nurse. Being both from the Northeast, Lily, a Naga, and I, a Manipuri, bonded very well. She invited me over many times and fed me Naga smoked pork, fish steamed in banana wraps, chicken with bamboo shoot, and whatnot. One afternoon, she told me to meet her cousin, Ilemza, a handsome man of around my age, who worked as a voice and accent trainer in a call centre.

Having been single for many years, I finally decided to go out on a date with Ilemza. He was as expected a fine gentleman, caring, and smart. My relationship with Ilemza made me realize I could never love anyone apart from Som. Ilemza truly understood my side of the story and saved both of us from embarking on a sinking ship.

It was Ilemza with whom I shared the truth about Som. Som was not a man, and Som never died in an accident. Som was a young woman of twenty-five, full of life, a rebel who picked up arms against the state. It was on July 23, 2015, that Som was arrested by a combined force of the army and the state police after hours of firing. She was the only female rebel, the rest were all male. The next day, local dailies reported,

"9 UGs, including one female killed at Moirang in an encounter."

The eyewitnesses had a different story to tell.

"Hold me tight, the roads are bumpy."

I was ultra-cautious as a pillion rider and we took the long-abandoned stretch nearby the Baruni hills. It was dusk, the sun was setting in behind the hills, Som and I decided to rest under the tree in the nearby field. She pulled my left hand towards her and I pulled her lips towards me. There was no one around, just the two of us, in this quietest corner of the earth.

"How is darling Alberto's flower?" She grabbed my waist.

"The real Alberto doesn't have one."

The next moment, she was in between my thighs. Her silky hair rubbing against my smooth and fair skin and her tongue probing each corner of my flower. I burst myself into a fountain only for her mouth to catch each drop of it.

It was on a heavily raining day on July 26, 2015, I rushed to the morgue with my brother to identify the dead body. After much hassle with the security guards, we were finally allowed to see the body. The post-mortem report said she was sexually assaulted and shot multiple times. Her innerwear had semen and blood stains and her entrails were out. In March 2016, after nine months of massive protests, there was some semblance of hope. Som's family refused to take any monetary compensation from the Government. They wanted a proper trial to prove that it was an extra-judicial killing. A commission headed by a retired judge was formed to investigate the matter and the report is yet to be submitted even after four years.

"Baby, when you are away, how will I spend my days here? I will join a college nearby."

The nearest college was more than a hundred kilometers away and Som's parents had already planned to send her to Delhi to study and prepare for future competitive exams.

I get down from my bed and walk towards the balcony. It's a pitch dark night in pin-drop silence. I check my phone, eight hours before my next shift. But I will not sleep tonight. So many people are suffering, so many lives have been lost. And what are these mindless attacks on Northeast migrants? Do I reconsider going to work tomorrow? Shall I be spared because I look after the sick and the miserable?

It's about ten yards from my home. As usual, Som dropped me there that day.

"Give me a goodbye kiss?"

"No, I won't."

"Are you scared of others?"

"No, I am only scared of being left alone. A life without you."

I hugged her tight and in that moment, two became one. As she whisked off of the alley on her motorcycle, I stood there until the motorcycle sound faded into the stillness in the air.

Flight

Miriam Aurora Hammeren Pedersen

The ropes just tied were abruptly cut
Those vistas of life are still so far ahead

Time is moving too fast
Yet everything is standing still

Six months since I felt your touch, my love
Six months since I saw your face and felt your breath

I was just thinking
Of all the things we've been planning to do
All the places we've been planning to go
Our favourite lesbian bar had to close for good
But we have other places

We have each other

I was just thinking
Of the smell of morning coffee brewing
Of chilling like in our bed at night
With dark stout and dark chocolate
You and me and Meow-Meow

I was just imagining
What it would be like
To feel your skin against mine again
To hold your hand
One more time

How am I supposed to tell you
That the borders closed again
And the airline just cancelled my flight

Poems for Anurag

Samudranil Gupta

I fell in love during quarantine with Anurag, who lived 1,250 km away from me: a distance more than safe to avoid transmission. But Anurag became my weakness, the reason for my breathlessness, my anxious insomnia, as I spent my days and nights confined in a room, stalking him on social media, watching his pictures again and again, and texting him with an obsessive zeal, in hope for his replies. I was sick with love, and there was no remedy.

There was no remedy for the virus either. Scientists across the world were working on building potential antidotes while people died in hospitals, on the streets, in their homes. Various governments issued surveillance protocols and severe regulatory measures to curb the spread. Police beat up everyone they found on the road for breaching the law. All that while, my heart, mind, and flesh remained under Anurag's spell. He was a lingering absent presence in my room throughout the quarantine:

Serotonin

One day, you will come to my house,
there will be eggs and beer in the freezer.

In the washroom,
water will spill out of the bucket,
I shall miss my 7 a.m. shuttle,

we will sit on the sofa,
watching a hockey match,
and cheer for the losing side.

Together. Very close.

My first poem for Anurag, named after the happy hormone. Written sometimes in July 2020. It could be raining outside. I was sad, and in need of serotonin. Due to his interest in neuroscience, Anurag used to post about hormones on his social media handles.

He thought love was more biological than emotional. What a prosaic thing to say – I would retort, but eventually give in. The words "s e r o t o n i n" or "d o p a m i n e" began to sound lyrical, because those were shared by Anurag. Those were *our* words. Hence, I chose this word for the title of my poem. Writing poetry for Anurag was the only way to touch him and feel him.

This was the same technique adopted by Italian filmmaker Alice Rohrwacher for her eight-minute-long lockdown film *Four Roads* (2021). In this short film, Rohrwacher used her camera to imagine an alternate form of establishing contact with neighbors. She zoomed in, from a safe distance, on the faces, houses, pets and orchards of her neighbors, thereby creating an experience of visual tactility. She also added a running commentary on the pandemic situation, her neighbors, and life in general to put the scenes in context. The film became a speculation on harmony and community at a time of isolation and estrangement.

When I kept writing for Anurag, I tried to include references of things that surrounded me. This was because I tried seeking him everywhere and in everything: the table-fan, the creases on my bed, the gap between the curtain and the windowpane. This was my method of manifesting him through day-to-day objects and integrating him with the banality of life. Thus, I grew more intimate with his absent presence. The pain of longing translated into a pleasure of pursuit. The second poem came (August 2020) when I was preparing breakfast in the kitchen, alone:

Cornflakes Bowl

Few people have this cornflakes-
bowl-ness about them. They are
like the mellow tapping sound
we hear when cornflakes rain on
the ceramic. Or the frothiness,
when milk is added, tiny bubbles
forming on white, marked by crusty
yellow, half submerged now, of the flakes.
The mixture is suddenly invaded by red
and blue of frozen berries, the brown
of honey, and almonds:
An aroma of warmth is born.

In her film, Rohrwacher pointed out several virtues she learnt from observing her neighbors from a distance: grace, resilience, affection, and labor. What did I learn from writing for Anurag? Creativity, and that it stems from deprivation. I learnt about love and longing too. I realized more than ever before that love and longing were complimentary. I still did not know when we could meet, if at all, as the pandemic and the quarantine continued. Therefore, writing for Anurag became a refuge for me. I was writing as a means of emotional survival. I was writing as a substitute for touch. And Anurag was the inspiration for these writings as well as their creative outcome. These poems happened because he was not there. He was always there because of these poems:

How Do I Love You?

I wear shirts of your favorite color.

I put on the perfume you told me about,

every time I step out,

alone.

I like everyone who comes from

your city to mine,

as if they are my blood brothers,

and ask them about the trees,

the status of traffic, and law and order

in your hometown.

I want to extract you from
irrelevant information.
I want to find you like a meaning
out of a poem.
I want to meet you at protest sites,
in cinema halls,
at gardens and parks that punctuate
this city –
                    this city without you.

I have written several poems for Anurag since 2020. Most of these poems, like the one above, written sometime in April 2021, are set outside the room, or replete with references associated with the outside world. The only exceptions are the poems titled 'Cornflakes Bowl' and 'The Smell Of Someone' (included below). Anurag and the outside world were no longer different. Both were unavailable. The poems were wish fulfillment. By this time, Anurag and I had started conversing over the phone. I was so delighted when he responded for the first time and wanted to continue the conversation. A ray of hope. But there were days Anurag would not reply to me, nor pick up my call, or he would go into a phase of prolonged silence. The quarantine had its strange effects on everyone. I wrote more profusely on those days. I would feel more confined, sicker, and more creative:

Touch Me

Touch me,
And I shall break like a wave on the shore.

*****

The Smell of Someone

Smell is a kitchen door
visible from the master bedroom:
it is a square within squares
of doors we pass through,
it is temporality,
it is space.
Smell is a pillow left untouched,

or abandoned.

Smell is memory of flesh.

Smell is memory of the unseen.

Smell takes over the room

after breaking is complete.

*****

Maybe He Smells of Rust

He smells of old windows:

rust.

A smell that retains

a part of the open sky and air,

and the memory of windowpanes,

creaking.

A smell so fragile that it

disappears

once it becomes familiar.

These three poems were written during the second phase of the quarantine. I wrote them while waiting for Anurag's texts. But he would not write to me. On those miserable days, I could not overcome my insomnia in any way. I felt relentlessly anxious, and words flooded my mind. I wanted to stand under the shower until the water ran off. I craved for a forgiving, lenient, and affectionate embrace. But all I could afford was to write. After a few weeks, he would remember me again, send me kind notes, and his pictures. I would not know what to do with that sudden abundance. On those happier days, my words disappeared.

A Queer Narrative

Morgan Easterly

On March 13th, 2020, I visited a new city for the first time. Previously, I'd been to a few tourist locations on the East Coast but never this far north. Those other trips were only for a quick getaway or a close friend's wedding, but this one, to Boston, Massachusetts, was acutely important for me. I had been accepted into a PhD program in the field of my choosing, the mode that turned the key in the lock of my mind: literature. The other, standard (although entirely novel to me) in-person trip was booked for Seattle, Washington, another city I'd wanted to visit (and still do), but recently and swiftly required cancellation for a rather "queer" reason: Seattle suddenly became one of the first major cities in the US to host a previously unheard of global super-bug. When I got the email saying I would need to cancel my plane tickets for the following day and instead meet a group of professors and prospective graduate students on a web app called Zoom, I began to wonder if anything in life, on a level simultaneously spacial, emotional, and sociopolitical, would be the same. Was this the brave new world? Is each "brave, new world" just a reinterpretation of one previously imagined and interpreted? When my husband and I arrived in Boston from Dallas, Texas, for a different and now somewhat concerningly in-person prospective student visit, the airport air felt sticky with residue, the permeating gasses' thickness phantasmagoric and dank, teeming with the dead skin cells of the past. We hopped in an Uber with apprehension and excitation and listened to the Governor declare a state of emergency while the driver took us to our Airbnb and talked to us about how he wound up in this foreign city.

It wasn't just the air – it never is – everything was heavy. The driver dropped me off at a local dive to meet current students in the program. I sat in confusion while each person around me lowered their neck in quick succession like a falling set of dominoes to read an incoming email declaring that classes would now and at least for the foreseeable future be held online effective immediately. Everyone quietly and perhaps affrightedly wondered if and when other prominent schools, possibly more, would do the same. What exactly were we all dealing with? I walked back to the rental with a current student who was kind enough to try and translate the lived experience of a humanities graduate scholar to someone who spoke a different language and then opened the door into an apartment that felt like an art installment about ambitious precarity, the place my husband and I booked to sleep. The difference between that apartment and the one we lived in together felt unwonted but thrilling. I could picture the two of us living there if we could afford it, but the space felt both unattainable and imperfect, just like the world surrounding it.

For the rest of this narrative, I will use the name Olivia to refer to the person who was once my husband but began her transition into womanhood shortly after moving to Boston. I must add that I hesitate to call this a narrative at all. The mere act of putting my experience to words, thus internally narrativizing, thus attempting in vain to reverse engineer a cohesive history from fragmented lived experiences existing both within and without me, some sort of linear progression, a story, belies pestilent misrecognition and misinterpretation that speaks to the dangers inherent in using language.

When I was a little girl, according to my mom and as evidenced in a photo my grandma liked to show me, I befriended a little boy with blonde hair and blue eyes. He was the only pre-K student who experienced terrible separation anxiety from his mother. He flew into screaming fits when she left him there to play with the other kids and talk to the teacher for the day. Legend says I took it upon myself to comfort him, and it worked; my grandma claims that at first, I would rush to comfort him and try to distract him from his fears, but eventually, he didn't need me to comfort him anymore because when he saw me, his crying stopped. He saw his friend and knew he was safe. In the photograph, we smile and hug; sometimes, I think I remember.

The blonde hair and blue eyes initially took my attention to Olivia when I met her on the first day of classes during my freshman year of undergrad. It seemed like a novel combination, a genetic jolt of some sort, and blue eyes always struck me as peerless. My father has blue eyes; the left one holds a burnt-orange fleck on the bottom right, his left and right, my right and left, respectively. Olivia's eyes are a similar shade of light blue *sans* fleck. They were kind eyes, a feature I keenly notice before determining whether I want to bore someone for depth. There was depth behind Olivia's eyes, a depth we shared in spirit tucked away within some floating kindred ether. I remember explaining to a close friend what our first interactions were like, "it was as if our souls were speaking to each other" is all I knew to say to communicate the affective experience. How does one explain something that makes sense to you to someone who has already determined it senseless? Many didn't understand why we coupled together. Olivia and I couldn't cognize each other's pain, but we knew it existed, and we knew it was more than what each of us individually knew it was and certainly far more than anyone outside of us knew it was. They didn't see; they didn't care; they would never understand, but she and I would try together to work toward a life that felt like home.

I met Olivia while in a dark place, desperately trying to escape a darker one. My home, the house my immediate family had lived in since I was thirteen, had been my lion's den. All of the homes previous to that had been, too. I had to get out to survive, but I had no idea how and getting into college felt like continuing my life in an improvisational play where I was the protagonist no one wanted. Socioeconomically, I wasn't supposed to attend an overpriced private Christian university, let alone pursue an undergraduate degree. Psychologically, I wasn't supposed to stay on an ideological trajectory to which I patently did not belong – in this, Olivia and I were similar. We became immediate friends. Then, we somehow fell in love in inexplicable and maybe even novel ways, or what I imagine being love. Love is the thing you cannot give, the thing you must have, the thing you can never fully receive. In the lived moment, it is everything, and upon the hindsight of historicizing narration, nothing.

I didn't feel unconditionally loved and safe at home; I often felt like an unspeakable obscenity. Abusive homes do this. Like queerness, they mar, otherize and villainize you. They form you into a lived image of everything that is supposedly evil within the world and blame you for man's heinousness, thus scapegoating you into the past, within the present, and out into the future. Abusive homes also, like quarantine, isolate you. They make you alone with yourself both physically and psychically. Isolation plus reflection can become singularity, which can feel like clarity, which can then narrate itself to you and change the way you think, followed by how you behave. My father, blinded by some mixture of religiosity and pride, persistently antagonized me in ways I don't want to discuss here. My mother's hurtful unavailability amid her own troubles took shapes I won't trace here. How do you describe something so affectively real, so bone piercing, so internally well-trodden, to someone who has never experienced it for themselves? I didn't think very highly of myself, and I noticed each and every way others, even those we are told should intimately care about you, didn't either. I didn't have bruises I needed to try and cover at school, something that happens to some; I had a transparent encasing that kept me perpetually distanced, detached, enclosed, but also displayed, gazed at. The gaze's heat took so many forms when it touched me. I always knew God's providence allowed it; I thought perhaps He watched; I always wondered if He was entertained. Who can know the mind of God? Many claim to, just like many claim to know the mind of another.

My mind determined that at 20, I would marry Olivia in our local, evangelical church home. I grew up attending a Southern Baptist church in a small Oklahoma town three times a week. The house I grew up in was intensely religiously fundamentalistic, and, again, I cannot say enough here. Even after leaving to find my own way, the idea of a church community pulled me in like a deceptive devil; pastors like to continuously remind their congregation that the devil is beautiful to both instill in them the idea of evil's alluring nature and to taint with fetishistic obsession what should instead remain beatific. The church as an institution gave and took so much of me that often I don't know where I begin and it ends. I don't know where the ideological evenness between the church as I knew it and my family's interpretation of it as it was imbued into me begins and ends. Even after my present graduate studies have determined the impossibility of a unified Self, I still attempt to extrapolate some set of bodily occurrences into a formal category, say, pathologies, and lose myself trying to trace back origins like language, begging for some initial signifier to assign myself an identity. I spent my wedding day weeping and didn't know why. I knew. When I pictured Olivia and me together in my mind's eye, I knew I could project into the future but never picture us into old age. I knew, but I didn't know. I still know, but I don't know. I know of the impossibility of knowing and yet feel the intense friction pressing me.

The thing is, we needed each other to survive, and we understood one another in a way that helped us do just that and even a bit more; we felt at home with each other like we never had. We could build a narrative together out of our otherness that resembled cohesion and, if we were lucky, feel like we were living the life we desired.

The year 2020 was the year I gained acceptance into PhD programs so that I could, for what felt like the first time, and perhaps was, pursue an end that nourished me. It was the year I signed 'sight unseen' paperwork for an apartment across the country and moved; it was the year I began my graduate studies to invest in myself. It was the year I decided it was necessary to confront parental abuse after receiving a phone call from one of my brothers, the tenor of his voice as I picked up the phone and heard him say, "dad tried to beat me up," struck a reverberating chord inside me that still rings. They didn't respond well, one not at all; I realized I finally knew that my thorn-in-the-side-hunch was correct, that I had already been rejected by them a long time ago. The year 2020 was the year I decided none of this shit was okay. It was the year my husband ventured through a dark night of the soul and came out the other end to inform me that she finally recognized her identity as a woman.

The year began with an air of new life tinged with death and demanded sacrifices. It demanded I put away narratives others violently imposed upon me. It required I do something else instead. Olivia and I knew we had done all we could for each other as a unit, and our realizations had a pungently bittersweet aftertaste. Although one is never truly whole, we had previously been even less, and while the news of her transition destabilized me, the freefall felt anticipated. We had spent a decade negotiating our queerness with the world; this information wasn't new. The only newness was how we would be interpreted. Would the world accept Olivia's reality? What would it think of my history and desires? We determined to separate and divorce but continue our spirits' fellowship in the unrecognizable ether. We consider each other kin. What is queer? What is a narrative? These answers I can only fleetingly assume and later recognize in their moments of alienation, of otherness, where I can trap an occurrence, force it into quarantine, and subject it to analysis. When doing so, I see the imperative to maintain unintelligibility. Marking a thing as known and subjecting it to the violence of a name, a definition that strictures, only limits and thrusts us into the danger of narrative, of believing we know the mind of the Other, the mind of God, the original signifier of all language.

Unbearable otherness drives the subject into fantasy. For both Olivia and I, it had been impossible to experience some form of sexuality when disassociated from our sexual organs in vastly different ways. It's challenging to endure individual lived experiences, so varied in the residue of interpretation they leave imprinted on our bodies and minds when inundated with authoritarian identifications. Quarantine forced self-reconciliation with the reality that there could never be an intelligible Self. The umbrella of "otherness" is not a vessel; it was never meant to hold things in place, keep them and name them. Instead, the umbrella and those under it can only act contrary to the outside; that is its most excellent function. When unexpected events unfold, they become the playing ground between politics and theory, affect and analysis. Multiple realizations meet, causing bodily discord. My life as a woman and self-identified believer in the equality of the sexes, races, and classes (feminist) brutally otherized me in a particular setting, and now a new setting forced bringing it to terms with an identity I did not have, that of transness. The fact of the matter is that these two identities did not need to fight and did not necessarily need to converge; they only needed to exist and remain both visible and accepted. To me, that is queerness: to cease adjudicating ultimately false 'truths' and to accept, or pursue a life in attempt to accept, living with negativity in its multifarious iterations across time and space. I would rather theorize than narrativize.

When Olivia began to come to terms with herself and shared her conclusions, it was no matter to me whether she was trans, non-binary, non-conforming, a lesbian, straight or any other sexual identification. She wanted to be called "she," she was attracted to women, and she wanted to be whom she believes she is. She is then that to me. My decision was shockingly instant and, at the time, felt simple in its obviousness yet disturbingly complicated in its ambiguity relative to outside readers. There are times when questioning and demanding answers destroys what should be kept ambiguous. Yet, like Newton's third law, every antecedent generates an equal or greater response, often in unanticipated directions, creating a grand divide between what we believe we desire and what we do when confronted with surprise.

I wanted a divorce; I was unhappy and had been psychologically sick with depression that wreaked havoc on my physical body and mind. We both slowly saw how we hid our true selves from each other and the world in hopes of being accepted by both the limitations of our conceptualization and the strictness of the world's ideological binarisms. Whatever sense of a Self I was going to live my life in pursuit of, whatever being-in-the-world I was going to do, could not continue in a system that did not match my love for the person. I felt drained of all life but without knowing what the life I had been drained of felt like. The affective love I had for her was not identifiable within the social-relational context of a marriage, a caring, committed partnership between counterparts, but instead an amalgamation of storge and pragma not alchemized in our current hegemonic culture. Olivia and I had to build a home for ourselves to live under, and it was a queer one. Our affective relationship, our love for each other, had no place within heterosexual definitions of communal love outside the boundaries of marriage. We had to nurture each other, and we wanted to; we built each other up and fed each other. When we got married, we both worked to help financially support the other returning to school to complete undergrad (in a carnivalesque turn of events I won't describe here, we both lost parental support the same year, thus forcing us to drop out of the University where we met). After graduating, she felt contentment with the life direction from her career, and I wanted desperately to keep the flavor of learning on my tongue; I needed to make a meal out of knowledge and feed myself.

The reflection my life required made me recognize the importance of community outside of dogma. My experience cannot be that of every religious individual, just as my experience cannot be that of every queer person, but between both the bounds of the Real, the bounds of language strung up in heteronormative ideological adherence and the vibrant other of the queer, there exists a gaping need for relational love. The limits of kinship from our current culture cannot contain everyone's needs, and so many have been displaced. We all need a space to participate in varying acts of love. When our world didn't offer us a foundation, we created a makeshift one with what we had outside the limits.

Otherness must preserve its sacred defiance in the face of normative, murderous hegemony. Affective and material liminality remains necessary for its function as the undoing of knowing, the defense against oppression that requires we lay down our demand for order. Identity creates marginalia; we don't have to deny identity, but we also cannot deny marginalia's existence as such, especially since they are not fully bought in on our cheap world of language. My life has been like queerness, nothing I foresaw, anticipated or imagined. Occupying the space of the other, the not-all that can never be feels like freefalling. Here in the present, writing a narrative on my life that feels and has always felt more dreamscape than physically spacial, I don't know what to say about the future. Ironies about anti-futurity aside, what is there to say I have learned? I've learned to know that you must always try to learn more but never arrive at a conclusion, a definition, a truth.

Queerness is the thing that invariably marks but can never be spoken. The narration task will only ever, at its least problematic, gesture toward the thing itself. Nothing I write down will communicate my experience. Life is flailing toward formation and inevitable failure; then, when we do not fully recognize it, it repeats itself to the same beat but a different tune, where we have the opportunity to pick it up. The question is what we then do. This new chapter in my life, this new repetition, has what masquerades as new knowledge, and I anticipate a new direction where the way is paved in the malleable sand. I'm going to continue pursuing my PhD because it is what drives me. I will desire a partnership built on mutual care, admiration, passion, and respect because it drives me. I don't pretend to know the end of these drives before the ultimate end.

God's my life, stolen

hence, and left me asleep! I have had a most rare

vision. I have had a dream, past the wit of man to

say what dream it was: man is but an ass, if he go

about to expound this dream. Methought I was—there

is no man can tell what. Methought I was,—and

methought I had,—but man is but a patched fool, if

he will offer to say what methought I had. The eye

of man hath not heard, the ear of man hath not

seen, man's hand is not able to taste, his tongue

to conceive, nor his heart to report, what my dream

was. I will get Peter Quince to write a ballad of

this dream: it shall be called Bottom's Dream,

because it hath no bottom. . . .

– Bottom (Shakespeare *A Midsummer Night's Dream*, 4.1.205-216)

Fruiting

Koyote Millar

Now I dream of oranges:

Firm flesh blushing hotly as I gently peel

bright-burnished armour, finding sweetness underneath.

Sun sliding off steep mountain slopes, dark groves of trees

with shiny leaves, cacophony of birds and bees and breeze.

Right here today the world is grey, a frozen waste.

But you just smiled at me, so now

I dream of oranges.

Contributors

Maisnam Arnapal is pursuing a PhD in Feminist Studies at University of California, Santa Barbra. He belongs to the Meitei Indigenous people from Manipur, India. His research looks at the queer and trans movements among the Indigenous peoples of Northeast India.

Celia Velo Camacho is a queer, non-binary person from the '90s. People think they are everywhere and can do everything, but they are actually a mountain leader, researcher, writer and cat parent currently based in Freiburg im Breisgau. In the village where they grew up, they are known as the child of the teacher Josefi or the child of Rapi's younger son, which is the alias of their grandfather. When they finished their BA, they started doing research about outdoor education. They are now finding new paths where they feel more comfortable, discovering queer pedagogies. During their days off they spend time cooking, traveling by bike and questioning themself in reading and writing, both poetry and prose.

Mie Cornoedus is a photographer who has lived in Indonesia (25yrs) and in South Korea (5yrs), but is currently based in Luxembourg. She has a long career of making her own work, both documentary and art photography. She set up her own studio in Indonesia where she runs a project on sustainable tourism, which includes an alternative art gallery, ViaVia Jogja. The gallery is well known for being a stepping stone into the art world for contemporary artists and curators. Mie has exhibited her work in solo and group exhibitions in Indonesia, Japan, South Korea, Norway, Belgium, France and more. Her website is: miecornoedus.com and her email is: viamie@mac.com

Morgan Easterly is a second-year PhD student in the Tufts English Department, Tufts University, Boston. She likes to think about critical theory, the parallels and simultaneity of literature and philosophy as well as feminist, gender, and sexuality studies.

Jonah Fedorowicz is a 30-year-old Latinx artist based in Stavanger. He is a transmasculine person preoccupied with accessibility and intersectionality issues in the international community. He hopes his art can contribute to the conversations at play. You can see his portfolio at: www.into-the-unknown.me and his email is: intotheunknowndotme@protonmail.com

Samudranil Gupta is a PhD candidate at New Delhi's Jawaharlal Nehru University. He also teaches writing and literature at O.P. Jindal Global University, Sonipat. He primarily identifies himself as a queer artist. Two of his poems were included in an anthology titled *Clouds of Utopia*, The Alcove Publishers, 2020.

Minal Hajratwala is the founder of the Unicorn Authors Club, a magical sanctuary where authors of color (and allies who really mean it!) finish gorgeous, urgently needed books. Her books include *Bountiful Instructions for Enlightenment* (poetry), *Moon Fiji* (travel), *Out! Stories from the New Queer India* (anthology), and *Leaving India: My Family's Journey From Five Villages to Five Continents* (nonfiction), which won four literary awards and was called "incomparable" by Alice Walker and "searingly honest" by The Washington Post.

Hansika Jethnani is a poet and visual artist. Her work explores a variety of themes including colonialism, migration, the stories of her ancestors, shame she has learned to carry, shame she is learning to unlearn, her body, her queerness, & everything in between. Her work has previously appeared in *Young Ignorantes, Whip Zine*, *Mush Stories, Chaicopy Literary Journal, United Nations Girls' Education Initiative, & Royal Museums Greenwich.* She is also a contributor to three anthologies, *Love As We Know It* (Delhi Poetry Slam), *Fearless Love* (Mohini Books), & *Raza: A Queer Poetry Anthology* (One Future Collective). She has previously performed at Battersea Arts Centre as part of the immersive theatre show *Rallying Cry* produced by Apples & Snakes. Sometimes she feels like a pink cloud.

Martine Johansen is a spoken word poet, novelist and editor. She debuted with the beat-inspired novel "Hvite jenter kan ikke synge blues" in 2015, and later followed up with the novels "Lykkelige mennesker har ikke bikkje" and "Vi har ikke fire nye år". She has also co-written a non-fiction book about spoken word called "Den store SLAM!boka". In 2016 she founded the queer publishing house MELK together with Anna Nafstad. Martine is currently working on a YA-book and teaching spoken word and SLAM!poetry to kids, youth and adults, both in Norway and internationally. She is a slam poet and board member in SLAM!kollektivet and active in SLAM!poet. She is also editor of the queer culture publication MELK, editor and advisor for Agenda teXt v/ Agenda X / Antirasistisk senter, and spearheading the campaign for a queer culture center in Oslo: Et skeivt kultursenter. You can find her at: www.martineslammer.com and on Facebook and Instagram

Koyote Millar is a poet, therapist and queer labourer of love based in Oslo, Norway. They aim to become richer and clearer with each new confusion. In middle age they know less and sense more. They listen, write and sing to acknowledge suffering and limitations, and invite joy and possibilities. You can run into them online, in print, on stage and in person.

Miriam Aurora Hammeren Pedersen (born 1990) is a white, neurodivergent, lesbian transgender woman from Norway. She holds a PhD in social anthropology from the University of Cape Town, South Africa, and is currently working in the field of LGBTQ+ education and advocacy. Miriam has written extensively on feminism and minority topics in various contexts, and her poetry collection "En Balansert Debatt" was published in 2022 by queer publishing house littMELK.

Anil Pradhan (he/him/his) is a doctoral candidate at the Department of English, Jadavpur University, Kolkata, India, and his research focuses on the intersectional politics of sexuality, home, and memory in contemporary Indian queer diasporic literatures and cultures. Complementarily, through his poems, he has been able to share how finding home and coming to terms with and celebrating one's queerness can often be synonymous. This intimate context has been reflected in his first book of poems titled *flitting oddments* (2020), published by Writers Workshop, Kolkata. His creative works have been published in *Visual Verse: An Anthology of Art and Words*, *Café Dissensus*, *In Plainspeak: A Digital*

Magazine on Sexuality in the Global South, *The Statesman – Voices*, etc. He was selected for the 'Language is a Queer Thing' India-UK poetry residency, sponsored by the British Council, and was a visiting poet at the BBC Contains Strong Language Poetry Festival, Birmingham, both in 2022. He can be contacted at pradhan.anil7@gmail.com.

Anwesh Sahoo is a Visual Designer, Technical and NFT Artist, the first Indian recipient of the Troy Perry Medal of Pride for compassionate Activism, the youngest winner of Mr. Gay World India and creator of 'The Effeminare'. With features in Vogue, Rolling Stone and the Hindu as a breakthrough queer artist, he has taken on the stage of TEDx as a speaker asserting the need to celebrate gender as a spectrum. He blogs and draws at The Effeminare, a parallel universe where he gets to illustrate the Utopian world he wants to be a part of. He looks at life as a thrilling mystery novel written by God and, since his novel has only started, he'd go with: "I am still evolving".

Rahul Sen is a PhD Candidate in the Department of English at Tufts University, Massachusetts. His areas of interest include psychoanalysis, queer theory, literary studies, and cinema studies. Rahul loves to drown himself in the melodramatic, romantic, and sleazy world of Bollywood films. He thinks that the magical power of love can change ourselves and change the world!

Subhajit Sikder is a Dalit queer research scholar, activist, painter, and digital artist. He is pursuing MPhil/PhD degree at the Department of Media and Communication, London School of Economics and Political Science. He is interested in studying how contemporary social media visual forms represent, subvert and problematize experiences, identities, subjectivities, and realities. Subhajit is a trained painter, learning painting since the age of 7. He also creates memes that often attempt to problematize dominant gender and queer politics, social media subjectivities, and contemporary politics.

Asad Ali Zulfiqar is a Karachi-based artist. They're the recipient of the Prince Claus Seed Award 2022. They received a BA in Communication & Design from Habib University in 2020. In their art practice, they use text, image, and sound to elevate the mundane and explore compassionate, possibly playful ways of looking at times with intentionality.

*

Mohini Books is an Oslo-based, queer-centric publisher. We have previously published *Taste & see: A queer prayer*, *Fearless Love: Anthology*, and *Becoming Buddha: Meditations.* Mohini Books takes its name and inspiration from the Indian myth of Mohini, a queer story which celebrates the diversity of genders and sexualities, a playfulness, and a subversive spirituality.

www.mohini.no

www.ingramcontent.com/pod-product-compliance
Ingram Content Group UK Ltd.
Pitfield, Milton Keynes, MK11 3LW, UK
UKHW022000190726
13853UKWH00004B/1632

9 788293 637080